I'm a Manatee

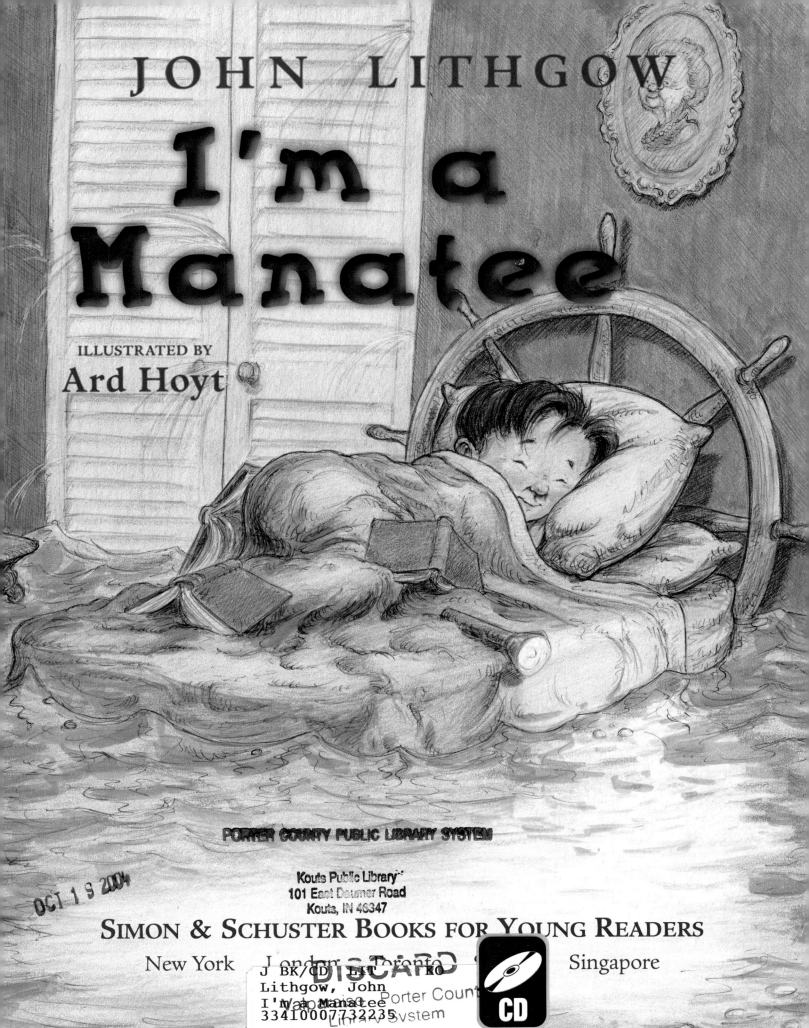

JOHN LITHGOW

I'm a Manatee

ILLUSTRATED BY
Ard Hoyt

SIMON & SCHUSTER BOOKS FOR YOUNG READERS

New York   London   Toronto   Sydney   Singapore

From time to time I dream
that I'm a manatee,
Undulating underneath the sea.

Unshackled by the chains of idle vanity,
A modest manatee,
That's me.

I look just like a chubby brown banana-tee
As I nose along the cozy ocean floor.
Immune from human folly and inanity,

That's why a manatee
Is such a happy herbivore.

I'm a manatee,
I'm a manatee.
I'm every bit as wrinkled as my grann-atee.

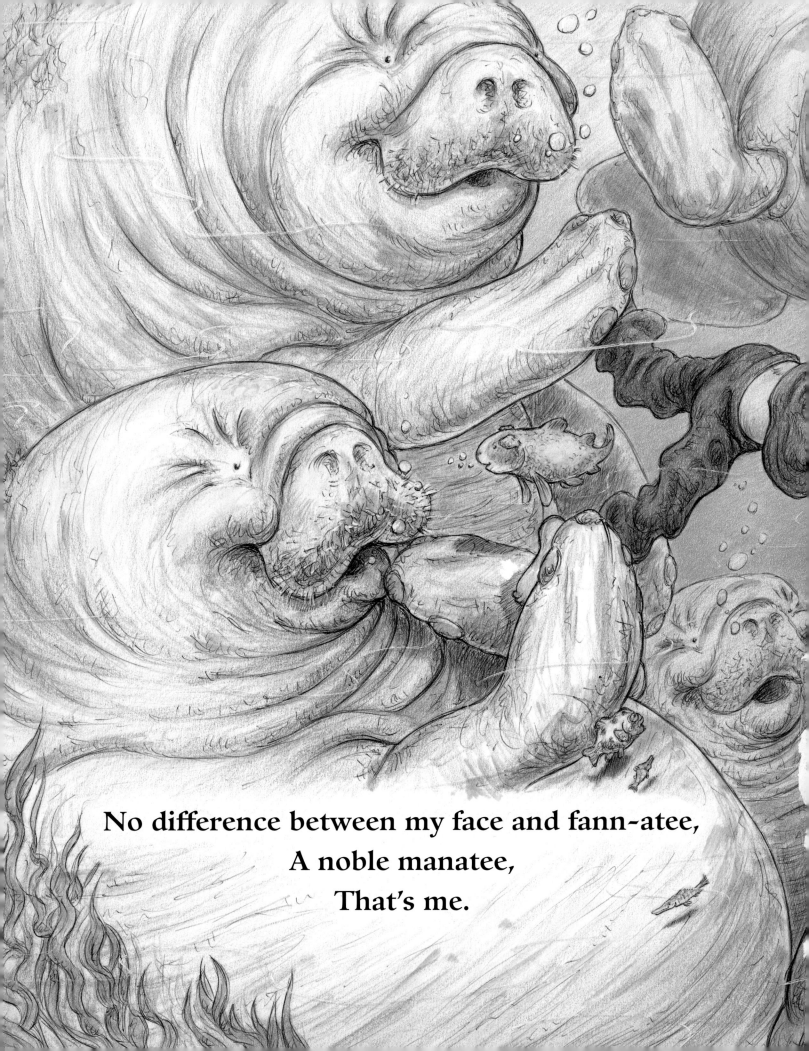

No difference between my face and fann-atee,
A noble manatee,
That's me.

With the dietary habits of a manatee,
I never fail to lick my platter clean.

I sprinkle seaweed on my Raisin Bran-atee,
The perfect manatee cuisine.

With my wit, sophistication, and urbanity,
I dignify my watery domain.

No one near will ever hear me use profanity,
Because a manatee
Has his image to maintain.

I'm a manatee,
I'm a manatee.
I keep my reputation spick and span-atee.

No difference between my face and fann-atee,
A stately manatee,
That's me.

Encumbered by my lumbering gigan-atee,
I'm thought to be an ocean-going brute!

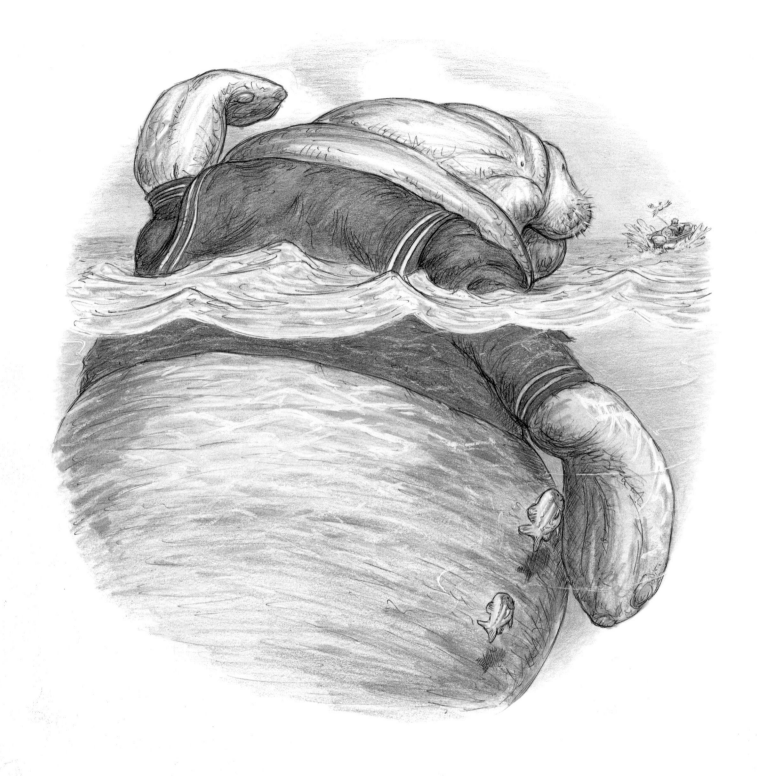

The least appealing creature on the planet-ee,

But to a manatee,
I'm cute!

I prefer my world of silence and of sanity,
But my underwater friends don't all agree.

For whenever I am dreaming I'm a manatee,
Somewhere a manatee
is dreaming that he's me!

I'm a manatee,
I'm a manatee,

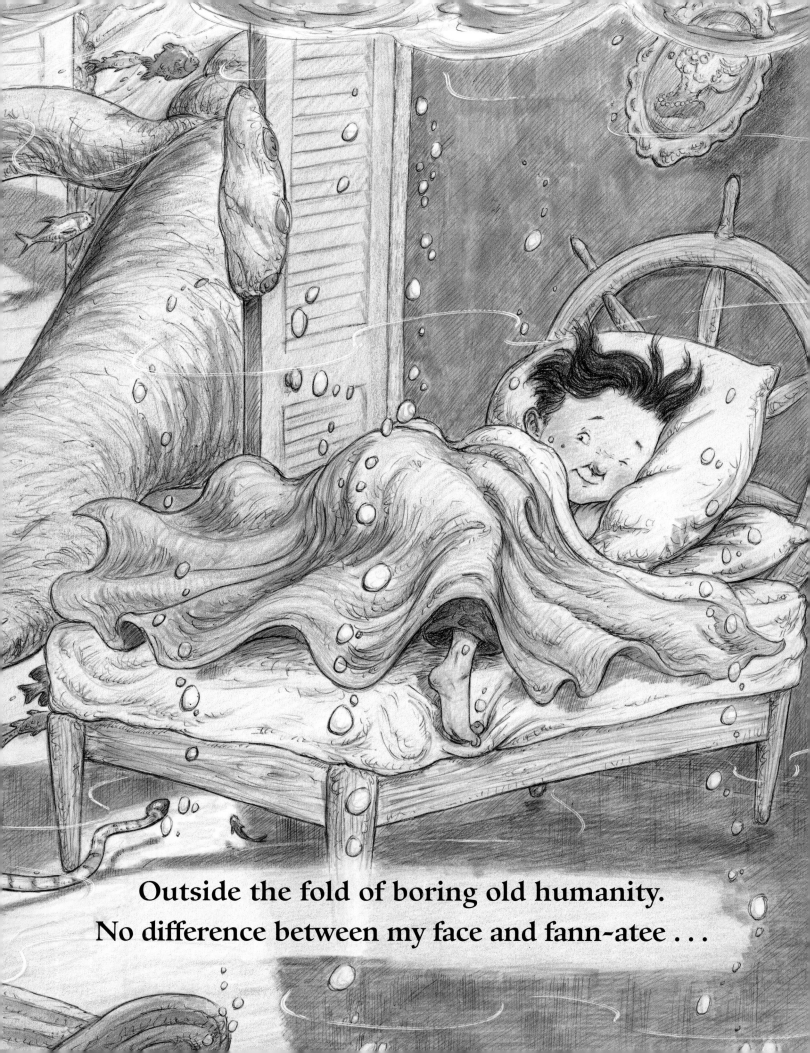

Outside the fold of boring old humanity.
No difference between my face and fann-atee . . .

I'm a roly-poly,
Jelly-rolly,
Sugar-bowly,
Heart-and-soully
Manatee . . .

That's me!

For my editor, David Gale—J. L.

To Mom and Dad—eternally glad I'm yours—A. H.

SIMON & SCHUSTER BOOKS FOR YOUNG READERS
An imprint of Simon & Schuster Children's Publishing Division
1230 Avenue of the Americas, New York, New York 10020

Book design by Paula Winicur
Score engraving by Robert Sherwin
The text for this book is set in Guardi.
The illustrations for this book are rendered in colored pencils, pen, and ink.

Manufactured in China
2 4 6 8 10 9 7 5 3 1

Library of Congress Cataloging-in-Publication Data
Lithgow, John, 1945–
I'm a manatee / John Lithgow ; illustrated by Ard Hoyt.
p. cm.
Summary: A boy imagines that he is a manatee, sprinkling seaweed on his Raisin Bran-atee
and dignifying his watery domain with his wit, sophistication, and urbanity.
ISBN 0-689-85427-7
[1. Manatees—Fiction. 2. Imagination—Fiction. 3. Stories in rhyme.]
I. Hoyt, Ard, ill. II. Title.
PZ8.3.L6375 Im 2003
[E]—dc21
2002004308